Other books by Asher Kite

Hazel Grey & Other Story (2020)

available from
INKFALL STUDIOS

Oil Town

Oil Town

by

Asher Kite

Oil Town

Cover art by Asher Kite based on
an original photo by Zukiman Mohamad

Deigned and published by

INKFALL STUDIOS

New Haven, Vermont

ISBN: 978-0-9965849-2-0 (hardcover)
               978-0-9965849-3-7 (paperback)

An earlier version of *Oil Town* was printed May
2017 and reprinted March 2019.

Written, edited, designed, and published
in beautiful Addison County, Vermont

Contents

Oil Town

Part 1: Oil Town

Oil Town

A clump of docks,
Centered in a sea of grey.
A black sky
coated in clouds.
Here we grow,
here we age,
here we die.
My name is Calvin E. A. Smith, and I
    am twelve.

Welcome to Oil Town.

My Family

In my family,
there are
my father,
my mother,
Daryl, my brother,
and me.

Our parents work, we go to school.

Mother says
we need to get smart,
so we can get to
the big city someday.

I hope we do soon.

Hurricanes

The sky is black and cloudy
most of the time.
Sometimes the clouds part
to show the stars,
and the moon.
But more often
the weather turns for a worse.
When the hurricanes come,
we have to scurry
to the nearest shelter,
and wait for it to go away.
They say in the big city they don't
    have hurricanes.

I would be glad to go,
I hate hurricanes.

School

They teach us
how the drills work,
how they were made,
the history of the drills,
why we use them,
and how we can't live without the drills.
I haven't studied something
besides oil drills in years.
My brother goes to a special school,
where they teach the engineering
of the drills,
and how we can make them better.

Our parents say that he is our ticket
to the big city.

History

In history today, we learned about how
there used to not be clouds overhead
all night,
every night,
and how people used to grow plants
in the soil, and in the sun.
I had to ask what they meant;
I thought humans had always lived
in the night,
in the dark.
No,
we used the live in the day,
the bright, sun filled day.
No one in my class has ever seen the sun.

Work

Daryl, my brother,
is on his last year of school.
Soon he will be sixteen, old enough
    to work,
and he will go to
the big city.
Then,
maybe
we will be able to follow.

Trouble

Our oil well broke down today,
in a hurricane.
It happens.

I will go to school
like normal,
but our parents will have to fix it.
If they can't,
we won't be able to deliver
the oil.

And if we don't deliver the oil
the provisions
will stop coming in.

Dawn

We are lost, my brother and I,
and we don't know our way back home.
We have to get back before dawn,
or we will fry
in the heat of day,
like fish on a grill.
As the clouds
were just beginning to glow,
and the humid air
began to heat,
we found our way back home.

We have lived here all our lives,
we shouldn't be getting lost anymore.

Solved

The oil well's fixed.
I knew they could do it,
mother and father.
I knew they wouldn't
make us lose our home.
I knew they wouldn't
make us fish for each meal,
and beg for shelter in another's shelter
as dawn became day.
I knew they could do it. Because if they
    didn't,
I knew we would never reach
the big city.

Fish

Fish are like the ocean;
uncontrollable and hard
to predict.

Fish are like
the night;
a constant
of our world.

Fish
are like oil;
a little
won't kill you,
but too much,
and you're
gone.

Death

Another one died yesterday.

I wonder
if he screamed and screamed,
but no one would let him in.

I wonder
if he ran past our shelter,
begging the door to open
as he burned in the sun.

I wonder
if he dived into the water,
in hopes of hiding from the heat,
only to drown in the murky depths.

I wonder
if anyone else cares.
This is why we keep on drilling for oil.
This is why we don't up and leave.

I wonder.

This Changes Everything

Daryl, my brother,
came home the other night
with a glint in his eye
and a smile on his face.

He explained
that the plans in his hands
changed everything.

He explained that he had found a way
to get energy from the light
of the sun in the day,
which would create as much energy
as
an oil drill.

The machine
he invented
could take every oil driller
off the docks,
and into

the big city.

Tonight he came home
with his eyes dull
and clouded,
and a frown
on his face.

We asked him if he had shown his plans
to the school administrators,
or the teachers.

He said
he had,
and that they had taken
his plans,
and put them into the incinerator.

We all realized then,
this changes everything.

Arguments

Daryl, my brother,
was yelling with my mother.
I heard them,
while I was at the door.

Daryl, my brother,
wants to create his machine.
But mother knows better.
If they find the machine,
we will be taken away,
and incinerated.

Daryl, my brother,
says once he gets to the
big city,
he will create his machine.
But mother knows better.

If he creates his machine
in the big city,
they will kill him, and

mother, father and me,
will never reach
the big city.

Graduation

Daryl, my brother,
is graduating tonight.
And tomorrow
he will be off to
the big city, in a boat.

I've never been on a boat,
they are expensive.

I hear once he reaches the main land,
Daryl, my brother,
will go on a train.

I've never been on a train,
they are expensive.

I hear once the train slows down at the
    final station, Daryl, my brother,
will be at
the big city.

I've never been to
the big city,
but I hope to soon.

Empty

One of the wells
in Oil Town
has gone empty.

The owners would have moved,
and their well would have been moved,
but now
there is nowhere else
to go.

I hope their souls
rest in peace.

The Letter

Daryl, my brother,
has sent us a letter from
the big city.

He says
he is doing as mother told him,
and that he is doing well.

He says
the big city is the most
wondrous place
he has ever seen.

He says they should put me into a
    special school,
so I will have a job when we come.
Mother, and father
agree,
so now I am being moved into a
    special school,
for who knows what.

Away from my friends,
away from my teachers,
away from my life.

But I will do it to get to
the big city.

The Cough

My father has a cough.
Cough,
cough,
cough.
All the time.
Every
single
night.

We tell him
to be quiet.
He begins to demand
respect, but a cough
chokes his throat
and pulls his words
away.

Last Year

The year went by.
People perished,
more oil
was tactlessly taken
from the earth.
Hurricanes caused
havoc to
each and every
one of us.
An oil well exploded,
dangerously dispersing debris.
Your average year
in Oil Town, except
this year,
father
was coughing.

School, Part 2

I was enrolled in an engineering school,
like Daryl, my brother.
And I went through school
and learned
how they make oil wells,
and how we
can improve their design.
I learned
the history of oil wells.
A thanks to the Chinese, and
thank you Edwin Laurentine Drake.
Who knows what our lives would be like
without the oil.

Another Letter

Daryl, my brother,
sent us a letter.
In it, he said
that he had
reached a stable enough
financial situation
for us to join him in
the big city.

Enclosed in the envelope
were tickets.

We are on our way now.

Part 2: The Big City

Boats

Adventure strikes me
like a cold and bitter wind from
     the north;
rare,
and quite bewildering.
No one is ever that excited
in Oil Town. But around me
people are smiling. Boats
have always been too expensive,
but mother, and father had enough saved
to ride the ferry.

Goodbye Oil Town,
I hope you burn.
I don't mean it.
There are some good people
in Oil Town,
but I hope the rest of them
burn.

Trains

The trains have air conditioning.
The air
is a cool 65 degrees
Fahrenheit, and
everyone here is rich.
I had never noticed
how shabby
and poor we look.
Swine who have broken out of our pen.
I have never seen a pig,
but there are some people
in Oil Town
who would qualify.

Waiting

Daryl, my brother,
is waiting for us
at the station.
I have no words
for how I feel.
I am free,
free from a system
which tries to keep the poor
poor, and the rich
rich. I am free,
into a world where it is okay
to have dreams.
I am free,
free from Oil Town.

The Doctor

Daryl, my brother,
takes us to see a doctor.
They test our lungs
for Advanced Smog Poison.
My lungs
are clean.
My mother's lungs
are clean.
My father's lungs
aren't.
They rush him away
to a hospital in the middle
of the city. It will cost a lot of money
to repair him. I don't understand;
we didn't mind him coughing
that much.

The Sun

The city is a giant dome
of a building,
completely air conditioned.
The sky is a blue screen
showing us what once was.
Throughout the day the yellow sun
moves across the sky.
Hour after hour,
day after day…
The fake celestial body mocking
the real people
going about their everyday lives,
or are the people even real?
Are we just dust floating,
pointlessly following our own
senseless goals in
hopes of reaching a better tomorrow?
Do we realize that tomorrow
will be the same as today,
the same as yesterday,
and the day before that?

Do our lives have
any meaning?
The Big City
is not
what I expected.

School, Part 3

They teach us geography.
Why do I care?
I'm never going
to Mexico,
or Canada.
I'm probably never going to leave
the city.

Why should I learn these things?
They will never
be helpful . . . I suppose the only reason
is to add extra work, more things
to remember, so we can fail
our tests in school, and curl
up and
die somewhere.

Something must be wrong with me.
No one is allowed
to talk about death in the Big City.

Shadows

Everything here
runs on oil. The cars,
the electricity, everything.
The smog is
sucked away, and fanned
outside of the city's dome.
The fans are run on oil.

The Hospital

They let us see father.
He is in a hospital bed,
with white sheets,
and a fake window
showing him a rolling prairie.
He looks sick. He didn't look
sick before he came
to the Big City.
He coughs, and I am afraid
he will explode.
A gas explosion
from forty years of smog,
all trapped in his chest.

They say he doesn't have long.

The Secret

Daryl, my brother, lets me in
on a secret.
He wants to build his
machine, but he needs
my help.
He says he wants to change
the world for a better;
clean of the skies
and the oceans, let people live
outside in the day
and feel the cool breeze
on their skin.
I tell him he is crazy,
and he is going to get us
all killed.
But I don't tell mother.

Light

They say
they can repair
father. Make him better
again. It will cost
ten times
our family's
annual income.
Mother
says yes. I think
we are going to get sent back
to Oil Town.

Work

Mother takes me
out of school, and tells me
to find a job.
I apply to a job in the hospital.

They say
no. I apply again.
They say
no. I apply again.
They say
"Rot in the streets you filthy liberal."

I am confused
and alarmed.
What is a liberal?

Trouble, Part 2

Mother
looks worried.

I had asked her
what a liberal was.
and now
she looks worried.

She asks me what I said
to them, and I repeat
"My father is sick.
I want
to be close to him,
I want to work."
Mother is confused
now too.
"What is a liberal?"
Bad,
mother says,
very bad.
Daryl, my brother, walks in.

Mother's face mixes
realization
with fear
in the most terrifying
manner.

Arguments, Part 2

They don't think
I can hear them, but
I can.
Shouting
just a room away.
Mother knows
Daryl, my brother, has
begun work on his machine.
Apparently,
the city police
are suspicious,
and our family
has been marked
as 'liberal.'
Apparently,
our future
is crumbling around us.

Darkness

Father
died today,
and they are charging us
in full.
I don't understand,
they said
they would repair him.
They said
they would make him better.
They said
a lot of things.

Things Get Worse

Daryl, my brother,
says they killed father, and
that they did it
because he is a liberal.
He blames himself, he
is in shambles.
I hate to hate him, but
the rest of us
are in shambles too.
And things get worse
when someone
comes knocking
at the door.

Trouble, Part 3

A woman, and a man,
in the black suits
await us
when we open up the door
to let in our demise.
They say
that they need to search
our place.
They do,
and they find
everything.
Daryl, my brother,
has plans
for his machine,
and even parts of the machine
hidden in his closet.
Our time
is running out.

Stupid Machine

The car is cold.
So very cold.
Maybe they like it that way.
The driver wears a golden watch.
It beats its spring-bound heart.
Stupid machine.
The car drinks the oil,
and coughs out
poison.
I don't think we are
too different.
Stupid machine.

Jail

We sit
and await
our impending doom.
We aren't together
but we each feel
the ticking seconds
of our lives
slowly
being burnt away
in an engine
of oil.

Judge, Jury, and Executioner

The judge:
a pudgy man
who sits in a high chair.

The jury:
a group of
angry looking conservatives
just waiting
to sentence
the liberal scum.

The executioner:
Time
will
tell.

Innocent

We are innocent.
Only Daryl, my brother, is a liberal,
and all he wanted to do
was help.

We are innocent
A mother and two teenage children,
desperately in debt, and
infinitely sorrowful for the death
of a family member.

We are innocent,
helpless citizens
who came to
the Big City in search
of a better life.
But here,
today,
in the great halls of the courthouse,
we are guilty.

Irony

We are being evicted
from the city.
They are going to drive us out
into the desolate wasteland
outside of the city,
and leave us there.

"It isn't murder,"
replies the smiling man.
"You're just being moved
to a more open living area!"
"It is murder,"
I tell myself
under my breath
"And you know it."

The Last Night

I find it hard to remember
that outside the city
it is night.

Here
they do a pretty good job
of faking the day.
The sky is a bright, bright blue,
and the sun is round
and yellow.
Neither are real.

How similar
to the hospital
and government
of the Big City.
Oil Town was bad,
but here
is somehow worse.

The World

The van is air conditioned.
How funny.
I will never
feel a temperature
this cool again
in the rest of my life,
although
that probably won't be very long;

I am fourteen,
but
when the sun comes up
I will burn
with my family.
We go together.
I am glad
father
is not wth us.

They say
we are here.

They send us
to the back
of the van,
into the heat-lock.
The doors to the world open,
and we all crawl out.

The van speeds away,
back
to the Big City.

At least here
we are free.

www.ingramcontent.com/pod-product-compliance
Lightning Source LLC
Chambersburg PA
CBHW070317120726
47910CB00007B/2525